GLOBAL HEROES
ARCTIC ADVENTURE

BY DAMIAN HARVEY

ILLUSTRATED BY ALEX PATERSON

MEET THE GLOBAL HEROES

MO
ANIMAL SPECIALIST

LiNG
ENVIRONMENTAL EXPERT

KEiRA
TECHNICIAN

RONAN

MATHS AND PHYSICS EXPERT

FERNANDA

TEAM MEDIC

THE GLOBAL HEROES ARE A GROUP OF CHILDREN FROM AROUND THE WORLD, RECRUITED BY THE MYSTERIOUS BILLIONAIRE, MASON ASH. FROM THE BEEHIVE, THEIR TOP SECRET ISLAND HEADQUARTERS, THEY USE THEIR SPECIAL SKILLS TO HELP PROTECT THE FUTURE OF THE EARTH AND EVERYTHING THAT LIVES ON IT.

For Vicky, with Love T.M.D. always
Damian

FRANKLIN WATTS

First published in Great Britain in 2022 by Hodder and Stoughton

1 3 5 7 9 10 8 6 4 2

Author: Damian Harvey
Illustrator: Alex Paterson
Series Editor: Melanie Palmer
Design: Lisa Peacock

A CIP catalogue record for this book
is available from the British Library.

ISBN 978 1 4451 8296 4 (pbk)
ISBN 978 1 4451 8632 0 (ebook)

Printed and bound in Great Britain by Clays Ltd, St Ives plc

The paper and board used in this book are made from wood from responsible sources.

FSC
www.fsc.org
MIX
Paper from
responsible sources
FSC® C104740

Franklin Watts
An imprint of
Hachette Children's Group
Part of Hodder and Stoughton
Carmelite House
50 Victoria Embankment
London EC4Y 0DZ

An Hachette UK Company
www.hachette.co.uk
www.hachettechildrens.co.uk

CONTENTS

CHAPTER ONE
KEEPING COOL

It was scorching hot outside the
Beehive, the Global Heroes' top secret
headquarters. Mo, Ronan and Fernanda
were with Professor Darwin, the scientist
in charge of the Global Heroes' gadgets,

helping test her latest invention. They had just finished running along a path that wound its way through the jungle, and now they were trying to get their breath back. "How were the thermo-suits?" asked the professor.

"They're really cool," said Ling.

"That's the idea," Professor Darwin replied. "They're designed to keep you cool when it's hot, and keep you warm when it's cold."

"A bit like a spacesuit," said Ronan.

"That's right," said the professor. "In fact, they've been made using spacesuit technology."

Mo wasn't impressed. "Do they really have to be bright red?" he asked. "Couldn't they be green or blue?"

"I'm sorry, Mo," said the professor, shaking her head. "But red it is."

"They need to be bright so the person wearing them stands out," said Ronan. "That way, if you ever need rescuing it'll be easy to see you."

"I hadn't thought of that," Mo admitted.

"Hopefully we won't need to put that to the test," said the professor. "But I would like to test the suits somewhere cooler."

"Speaking of cool," said Mo, "can we go back inside? I'm ready for a nice cold drink after all that running around."

"You can," laughed the professor. "But I'd like Ling and Ronan to do one more little run."

"No problem," said Ronan.

★★★

By the time they had finished, Ling and Ronan were exhausted. They were just taking off their suits when the alarm began to sound.

"A mission," cried Ling, excitedly. "I wonder what it could be this time?"

"We'll find out when we get up to the control pod," said Ronan. "I'll race you to the aqua lift."

"Hey!" cried Ling, running after him. "Wait for me."

The lift doors were just opening when the two of them got there. "I hope you hung those thermo-suits up," said Professor Darwin, stepping out of the lift.

Ling and Ronan looked at each other guiltily.

"The alarm started to ring," explained Ling.

"We'll go and do it now," said Ronan.

Professor Darwin sighed and shook her head. "Go and see what the emergency is," she said. "The others will be waiting for you."

"Thanks, Professor," Ronan called, as the lift doors closed between them.

When they opened again they could see the professor had been right. The rest of the Global Heroes team was already there.

Mo had his feet up, lazing on a sofa. Keira was sitting on a chair while Fernanda practised her bandaging skills on her. A huge television screen on the wall showed Mason Ash, the billionaire head of the Global Heroes, sitting in the shadows of his office.

"I wonder what he really looks like," Keira whispered.

"Who knows?" Fernanda whispered back. "We never get to see him properly."

"You'll all get to see me when the time is right," said Mason Ash. "But right now there's something more important I want you to look at."

The picture on the television changed and the friends found themselves staring at a snowy screen. At first, it looked as though it was just a photograph, but as they watched, two large shapes came into view.

"Polar bears," cried Ling. "They are so cute."

They watched as the bears walked across the screen then vanished into the snowy white background.

"They might look cute," said Mo, "but polar bears are the largest land-living carnivores alive today. They are at the top of their food chain."

"You're right," said Mason Ash. "But they are in danger of becoming extinct in the wild."

Mason told them that he wanted Mo and Ling to travel to the Arctic and find out what was happening to the bears. "Mo's knowledge of animals and Ling's environmental expertise will be essential for this mission."

"What about the rest of us?" asked Ronan.

"You and Keira will be providing important support from the Beehive," replied Mason. "Fernanda will be busy revising."

Fernanda nodded. "I've got my medical exam tomorrow," she explained. "So I'll have to sit this mission out."

Just then, Professor Darwin came into the room. "It sounds like we'll be testing the thermo-suits in a cold place sooner than I expected," she said. "As long as Mo doesn't mind them being bright red."

"I don't mind what colour they are now," he said. "We've got polar bears to save."

"There's just one more thing," said Mason Ash. "Make sure you keep your eyes open – I have a feeling you won't be alone out there."

"Don't tell me," said Mo. "Evilooters…"

"We're not worried about them," said Keira. "We've beaten them before and we can beat them again."

"I'm sure you will," said Mason. "But be careful. We can't predict what they'll get up to next."

The team had been in two previous encounters with the Evilooters:

In Australia, the Evilooters had been capturing wild animals so they could sell them for profit. They might even have been responsible for the bushfires that had swept across large areas of land. The fires had destroyed people's homes as well as the natural habitats of lots of birds and animals.

In Brazil the Evilooters had been making money by dumping plastic waste into the ocean. Plastic poisons the water and harms life in the ocean and on the land.

"They only thing they seem to care about is money," said Mo.

"And they are damaging the planet in order to get it," added Ling.

"One thing we don't know," said Mason, "is just how far the Evilooters are willing to go to get what they want. That's why you have to be so careful."

CHAPTER TWO
NORTH TO THE ARCTIC

After collecting their thermo-suits,
Ling and Mo headed up to the landing
pod where Professor Darwin was busy
refuelling the eco-boosters.

The foul smelling fuel made Mo pull
a face.

"It really is horrible," he said.

"It's made entirely from recycled
waste products," the professor reminded
him. "One tank of it is enough to carry
an eco-booster twice around the planet.
And it has zero carbon emissions."

"And reducing carbon emissions is
very important," Ling added.

"But does it have to be so smelly?"
asked Mo.

"I'll see what I can do," said
Professor Darwin. "But I'm not promising
anything."

"Thanks, Professor," said Mo,

climbing aboard the waiting craft. "You're the best."

As Ling and Mo fastened their safety belts, the roof of the landing pod began to slide open above them. "Looks like perfect flying weather," said Ling, gazing up at the clear blue sky.

Mo nodded but didn't reply. Something was clearly bothering him. "Don't forget your rucksacks," said Keira.

"We know," said Ling. "That way you can track us on one of your gadgets."

Keira held up her tracking device and gave a thumbs up. They all knew how much she loved gadgets, but they also knew how useful they were for their missions. Getting lost would be bad enough, but getting lost in the frozen Arctic would be much worse. It was good to know that Keira would be keeping track of them every step of the way. While she was doing that, Ronan would be kept busy carrying out any research that needed doing.

"Well, what are you waiting for?" said Professor Darwin. "The world clock is counting. You've got 48 hours to complete your mission."

As their eco-booster rose high into the air, Mo let out a long sigh.

"Are you worried about flying?" asked Ling.

Mo shook his head. Whizzing around
in the eco-boosters had seemed scary at
first but he'd soon got used to it. It was
all the talk of carbon emissions that was
bothering him. He knew reducing them
was important, but he didn't know why.

"Don't worry," Ling told him. "You can't be expected to know about everything."

"But everyone else knows about them," replied Mo.

"And you know all about living creatures," said Ling.

"That's because I'm interested in them," said Mo. "I tried learning about carbon emissions and stuff like that, but it just doesn't stick in my head."

"Don't worry," said Ling. "I'm sure we both have a lot to learn on this mission. We can help each other."

Mo smiled. It was good having friends like Ling and the others.

As usual, Professor Darwin had programmed the eco-booster to fly on autopilot. That meant there was nothing to do but sit back and enjoy the flight. Mo closed his eyes and imagined what it would be like to actually see a polar bear in the wild.

Ling and Mo were half asleep when Keira's voice came over the eco-booster's radio. "You'll be landing in a few minutes," she said.

"Everything's white," said Mo, peering through the eco-booster's canopy. "Is this the North Pole?"

"Not the North Pole," Ronan told him. "But you are in the Arctic Circle."

As the eco-booster went lower, they saw that not everything was snow and ice after all. Trees reached up from the frozen ground, their branches heavy with snow. Further ahead, in the distance, they could see a dark stretch of water too.

For a moment, Ling thought she spotted something else but they had flown past it before she could get a proper look.

"I can't see any towns or villages," said Mo. "Where are we going?"

"To an Arctic research station," Keira told them. "There are two Norwegian scientists there at the moment – Arvid and Karin. Mason says they'll help you as much as they can."

"That sounds cool," said Mo.

"That's not all," said Ronan. "We've been told there's a couple of polar bears near the station. Hopefully you'll get to see them as well."

Mo and Ling could hardly wait.
Now they were in the Arctic, the mission
seemed even more exciting than before.
Then Ling spotted something ahead of
them. "I can see the research station,"
she said.

As soon as their eco-booster
touched down, the two friends clambered
out and were met by the scientists.

"Welcome to The Arcturus Research Station," said Arvid, shaking Mo's hand. "Sometimes other scientists come and work here for a while," explained Arvid. "But for most of year, we have the whole place to ourselves."

"There is no one else for miles around," said Karin. "It is just us and the wildlife."

"That's right," said Arvid. "And the Arctic is home to some very unique wildlife."

Mo nodded enthusiastically and told them how keen he was to see as much wildlife as he could while he and Ling were there.

"Well, I am sure you will get to see some Arctic foxes and hares," said Karin.

"And in the ocean we have orcas and beluga whales," Arvid told them. "If you are lucky, you might see a walrus or two.

"That's great," said Ling. "But it's really the polar bears we want to find out more about."

"Yes!" said Mo. "And we've been told you often see a couple of polar bears right here near the Research Station."

Arvid and Karin looked at each other for a moment. Then Karin let out a sigh. "I am afraid we have bad news," she said. "Our polar bears have disappeared."

"Disappeared!" cried Mo. "But how can they have disappeared?"

"Come inside where it is warm," said Arvid. "We will tell you all we know."

CHAPTER THREE
THE SEARCH BEGINS

The Arcturus Research Station was made up of huge egg-shaped pods, linked together by connecting passageways. It stood above the frozen ground on metal legs, making it look more like a giant caterpillar than a building.

From inside, large windows offered views across the Arctic. At the top, an observation deck allowed researchers to study the night sky.

Ling and Mo found that the station had its own laboratories, a library, and a games room. There was even a small cinema.

"What do you do here?" Ling asked.

"Arvid and I are studying the effects of global warming," said Karin. "Other people come to study different things."

Arvid pointed out a photograph pinned to noticeboard on the wall. "That is Professor Emile Dax," he said. "He was studying polar bears."

"What did he find out?" asked Mo.

"We do not know," said Karin. "He did not talk much."

"He did not even tell us he was leaving," said Arvid.

"That's strange," said Ling.

Although talk of the mysterious Professor Dax was intriguing, Mo was more interested in hearing about the missing polar bears.

"Ah yes," said Arvid, nodding sadly. "That is also strange."

"We often saw them through the windows," said Karin. "But they have not been around since the thunderstorm a few days go."

"I didn't think you had thunderstorms in the Arctic," said Ling.

"They are rare," said Karin. "But with global warming they are becoming more common."

She told them the thunderstorm had
been so bad that it had broken off chunks
of ice from a glacier.

"They make it dangerous for
passing ships," she added.

"Perhaps the storm frightened the
polar bears away," suggested Ling.

"Or perhaps they have gone in
search of food," said Mo.

"You could be right," said Arvid.
"But we are still worried and do not have
time to go and look for them ourselves."

"I think that's where we come in,"
said Ling. "We want to find out what's
happening to the bears."

Looking through one of the
windows, Mo shook his head. "Finding
white bears in all of that snow and ice
won't be easy," he said.

"I think we have just the thing you
need," said Arvid, rooting around in a
storage cupboard. "Yes, here it is."

"The bears are wearing electronic
ear tags," explained Karin.

"You should be able to locate them

using this," said Arvid.

Ling looked at the gadget the scientist was holding. It was like an older version of Keira's tracking device. "Does it work?" she asked.

Arvid fiddled with the device until the screen lit up. "Looks good to me," he said.

Mo wasn't so sure. "It doesn't seem to be picking anything up," he said.

"Perhaps the bears are out of range," said Karin. "Professor Dax was always walking around outside with his tracking device."

"We'll give it a try," said Ling. "We can take the eco-booster."

"Good idea," said Mo. "Let's make a start."

"You need to be careful out there," said Karin.

"She is right," Arvid agreed. "The Arctic can be very dangerous."

"We'll be careful," said Ling. "We just want to find the bears."

"The bears are just one of the things that make it so dangerous," warned Arvid. "Do not get too close to them."

***

Ling started the engines of their eco-booster and took hold of the steering column. As they took to the air, Mo radioed the Beehive and told the others about the missing polar bears. He also told them about Professor Emile Dax.

"I wonder what he was doing there?" said Ronan. "It's a shame you didn't get to talk to him. "

"It's good to hear the bears are tagged," said Keira. "That should make them easy to find."

"That's if the tags and the tracking device are still working," said Mo.

"If not, we haven't got a chance. It will be like looking for a ... well ... a polar bear in the Arctic."

Ling concentrated on flying the eco-booster while Mo concentrated on the tracking device. They had been flying in silence for a few minutes when Mo let out a frustrated sigh. "Still no sign of life," he said, staring at the device's pale blue screen.

"We should probably turn back," said Ling. "I can see the ocean ahead of us."

"Just a bit further," said Mo, looking out through the eco-booster's canopy. "Polar bears like it near the coast." Suddenly, the tracking device let out a faint beeping sound. "I think I've got something," he cried.

CHAPTER FOUR
ON THIN ICE

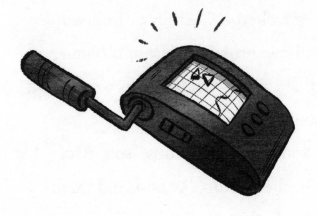

By the time they reached the edge of the ocean, the tracking device was beeping frantically, but there was still no sign of the polar bears.

"Perhaps they're in the water," said Ling.

"Or on one of those islands," said Mo.

"They're not islands," Ling told him. "They're icebergs. Chunks of freshwater ice that have broken off from a glacier or ice shelf. That's what Karin was telling us about."

"Some are enormous," said Mo.

On their radio, Ronan told them that only the larger ones were called icebergs. "I've just been reading about them," he said. "The smaller pieces are called bergy bits and the really small ones are known as growlers."

Ling pulled back on the eco-booster's steering column and the craft rose higher into the air. As it did, she spotted something. "What's that?" she asked.

"I think that's a growler," said Mo. Then his face lit up. "And I think there's a polar bear on top of it."

"A growler on top of a growler," laughed Ling.

"Ha, ha," said Mo, rolling his eyes. "Very funny."

"Be careful," warned Keira, over the radio. "They're dangerous creatures, remember."

"Don't worry," said Mo. "We'll keep our distance."

Ling flew them to a flat chunk of ice, close to the one the polar bear was on. "We should be able to get a good look," she said, as the eco-booster gently touched down.

The chunk of ice had a narrow section near the far end and they had to be careful stepping past it. "Watch where you put your feet," said Ling. "We don't know how thick this ice is."

They were quite close to the polar bear now and the tracking device had stopped beeping. Instead, it was letting out a high-pitched whistling sound.

Across the water the polar bear's ears began to twitch.

"Do you think it's all right?" asked Ling.

"I don't know," Mo replied. "Hopefully it's just sleeping."

Just then, a loud cracking sound filled the air. "What was that?" said Ling.

Before Mo had a chance to reply, the bear raised its head and let out a growling yawn. Then it slowly got to its feet and gave itself a shake. "The bear's all right," he said, excitedly.

"It doesn't look all right to me," said
Ling. "It looks angry."

As they watched, the bear shook its
head again and let out another growl.
"I don't think it likes the sound of your
tracking device," said Ling.

Mo switched the tracker off and the
annoying whistling sound stopped.

The bear stood staring at them across the stretch of water.

"I think we should head back," whispered Ling.

"I think you're right," said Mo. "Nice and slowly."

As Mo turned around he realised what had made the loud cracking sound they had heard. The ice behind them had broken and the bit they were on was drifting away. The gap between them and where the eco-booster stood was widening with every second. There was only one thing they could do.

"Jump!" yelled Ling, leaping across the gap and landing with a crunch on the

other chunk of ice. Mo was about to follow when there was a loud splash behind him. The polar bear had jumped into the ocean and was swimming towards them. Its huge front paws quickly pulled it through the icy water.

"It's coming after us," cried Mo.

He quickly took a step forwards and hurled himself across the gap. As his boots touched the ice, he felt it crumbling beneath him. "Help!" he cried, waving his arms around in the air, desperately trying to keep his balance.

Mo could feel himself starting to tumble backwards as Ling reached out and grabbed the front of his thermo-suit.

"Thanks!" he gasped, as Ling pulled him to safety. "That was close."

"Too close," Ling replied. "But we're not out of trouble yet."

The polar bear had already swum halfway across the water. Ling and Mo ran as quickly as their feet would carry them and reached the eco-booster just as the bear was heaving itself out of the water. As they took off, they could see the bear walking in circles on the ice below them.

"I didn't expect it to swim so quickly," said Ling.

"Polar bears are fast swimmers," said Mo. "But they prefer to wait for their prey to come to them. It must be really hungry."

"It nearly had us for its dinner," said Ling. "That was scary."

"That's probably enough excitement for today," said Professor Darwin over the radio. "You should head back to the research station for some rest now."

It was then that Mo realised something. "Oh no, the tracking device," he groaned.

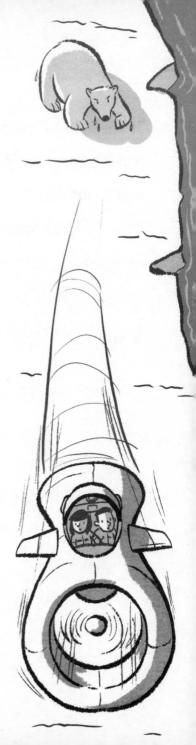

"I must have dropped it when the bear was chasing us. We'll never find the other bears now."

"Don't worry," said Keira. "I have an idea."

CHAPTER FiVE
A HELPiNG HAND

Back at the research station, Ling told
Arvid and Karin about their encounter
with the polar bear. Mo told them how
he had managed to lose their tracking

device somehwere.

"The important thing is you are both safe," said Arvid.

"That tracker was left by another group of scientists," said Karin. "They wanted to keep track of all the bears."

"Our interest is the effects of global warming," Arvid reminded them.

"Do you think it affects polar bears?" asked Mo.

"It affects everything," said Arvid. Karin told them that because of global warming, the Arctic Ocean was not freezing as early in the year as it used to. And the Frozen Arctic was getting smaller each year.

polar bear habitat over time

1980
2019

"That means the polar bear's natural habitat is getting smaller," said Mo. "They spend most of their time hunting on the frozen sea ice. Without that, it will be hard for them to find enough to eat."

Then, a large poster on the wall caught Mo's eye. He'd noticed it earlier but hadn't had the chance to look

at it properly. The poster showed an
illustration of the Sun and the Earth
alongside a picture of a greenhouse.

The greenhouse reminded him of the one
Grandpa Hamza had in his garden.

Mo nodded as he went over to look
at it. "The greenhouse effect," he said.

"That is it," said Arvid. "So you
know all about the greenhouse effect?"

Mo remembered Grandpa telling him that the glass in his greenhouse trapped the Sun's heat inside. It helped keep the greenhouse warm when it was cold outside. It was great for plants and vegetables but Mo didn't see what it had to do with global warming.

"Grandpa Hamza told me how his greenhouse worked," he said.

"It is the same with the Earth," Arvid told him.

"Carbon dioxide and other gases in the atmosphere act like the glass in a greenhouse," said Karin. "That is why we call them greenhouse gases."

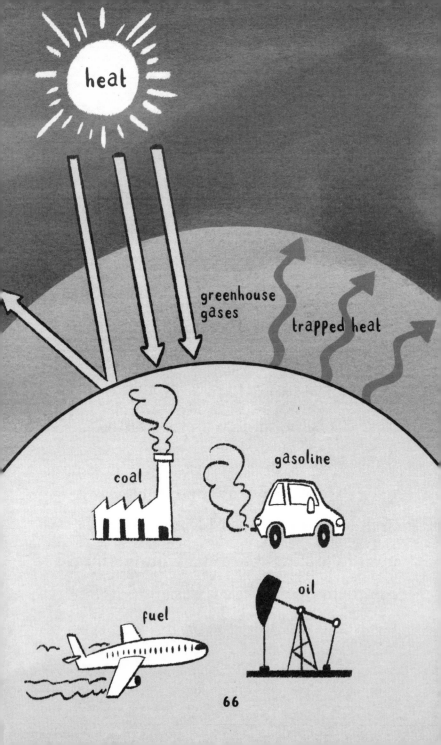

66

"It is like a blanket that keeps the Earth warm," said Arvid. "The Sun heats the Earth and the gases help keep the heat in. Without them it would freeze."

Mo was puzzled. "So if we need these gases in the atmosphere, why should we worry about carbon emissions?"

Karin told them that it was natural to have greenhouse gases in the atmosphere. He said that they started to become a problem when humans began

doing things that put
more carbon dioxide
into the atmosphere.

"Burning fossil fuels
like gas, coal and petrol
pollutes the air and increases
greenhouse gases," said Ling.

"That is right," said
Arvid. "It is like putting
on an extra blanket. They
make the world warmer
than it should be. The ice
in the Arctic melts and the
sea levels around the world
rise. Like I said ... it affects
everything."

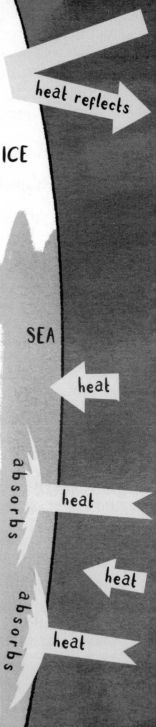

Karin explained that sea ice was so bright that it helped reflect the Sun's rays back into space.

"Without the sea ice, the Earth heats up even more," she said.

"We need to find out what else might be affecting the polar bears too," said Mo.

"I think you have both done enough for today," said Karin. "You should get some sleep and start again in the morning."

"But it's still light outside," said Mo.

Karin and Arvid laughed. "You are in the Arctic," said Karin. "It stays light for six months of the year."

★★★

The next morning, Ling looked through the window of her room. Outside she saw a second eco-booster parked on the ice. When she and Mo went to get breakfast, they found Keira waiting for them with a steaming mug of hot chocolate in her hands. She had been looking with interest at the noticeboard.

"I told Mason Ash that you might be able to use my help," said Keira. "I've brought my new tracking device.

Hopefully we can pick up the polar bear's trail again."

"That's great news," said Ling.

"We have more good news," said Arvid. "Mason kindly donated three new eco-friendly snowmobiles to help with our research."

"You can borrow them," said Karin, leading them outside. "They are great for getting around on the snow and ice."

"Wow!" said Mo. "I've always wanted to ride a snowmobile."

"They are fun, but one of our new snowmobiles has already gone missing," Karin explained. "Maybe Professor Dax has taken it."

"That's interesting," said Keira. "Professor Darwin says there's no record of a Professor Emile Dax."

"So who is he then?" replied Karin. "And what was he doing here?"

"We don't know that yet," replied Keira, "but I've sent a picture of him back to the Beehive. They'll soon find out."

"I bet he's got something to do with the missing bears," said Mo.

"You could be right," said Keira, "but there's only one way to find out."

CHAPTER SIX
TRACKS IN THE SNOW

The two snowmobiles whizzed across
the frozen ground, sending up a cloud of
snow and ice behind them. Mo sat behind
Keira with her tracking device in his

hand. Three green triangles in the centre of the screen showed where they were, but it was other coloured triangles he was looking for.

Keira had said blue triangles indicated some kind of creature, and red ones showed other people. Microphones in their helmets allowed the friends to speak to each other as they rode along. To communicate with the Beehive, they would have to use their radios.

"We're heading towards the coast where we last saw the bear," Ling said into hers. "The iceberg it was on was being carried away by the current."

"It could have come onto the

land by now," said
Professor Darwin.
"So keep your
eyes open."

"Keira says
her tracking device
should pick it up
before we see it,"
said Ling.

"Let's hope so,"
said the professor.
"Being chased once
by a hungry polar
bear is enough
for anyone."

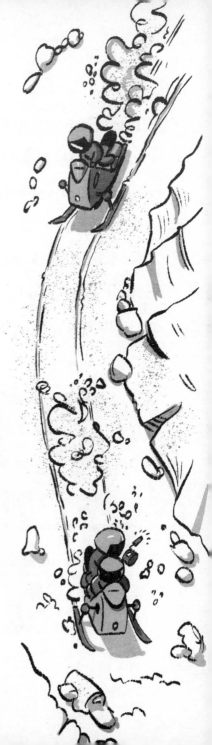

When they reached the ocean, Mo wanted to stop for a moment. "I just want to take a look," he said.

"What is it?" asked Ling.

"The sea ice," said Mo.

"What sea ice?" replied Keira.

"That's what I mean," said Mo.

"The Arctic Ocean should be starting to freeze by now, and it isn't. Global warming is definitely one reason why there aren't as many polar bears around."

"Well spotted," said Ling. "But there may still be more to it than this."

Mo got back on the snowmobile and Keira accelerated away, with Ling following closely behind. They hadn't gone far when the tracking device let out a beep.

"There's something ahead of us," said Mo. "I'm picking up two signals."

"What colour are the triangles?" asked Keira.

"That's the weird thing," said Mo.

"They're yellow circles."

"That must be the bear's ear tags,"
Keira replied. "We've found them."
The snowmobiles carried on and Mo
watched as the yellow circles on the
tracking device got closer.

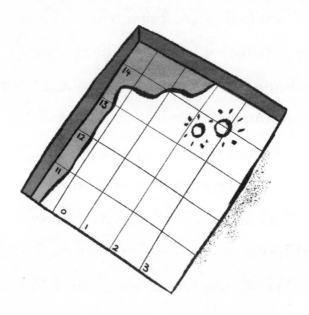

"We're almost there," he said.
"We should be able to see something
by now." Keira brought their snowmobile
to a halt and climbed off.

"Where are they?" asked Ling,
stopping next to them.

"According to the tracker, they
should be right here," said Mo.

"Perhaps it's not working properly,"
Ling suggested.

Keira took the tracking device
from Mo and fiddled around with it.
"I'm zooming in for a closer look," she
explained. "I should be able to pinpoint
exactly where the signal is coming from."
Without taking her eyes from the screen,

Keira took three steps forwards and then turned to her left. "Here!" she announced, crouching down and rooting around in the snow. When she stood up again she was holding something in her hand.

"The bear's ear tags," said Mo. "They must have fallen off."

"I don't think so," said Keira, examining the tags more closely. "It would be strange for two bears to lose their tags in exactly the same place."

"That means someone must have taken them off on purpose," said Ling.

"But who would do that?" asked Mo. The three friends looked at each other and all came to the same conclusion. "Evilooters!" they said together.

The Global Heroes had come across the Evilooters before. They were criminals who were only interested in making money, and they didn't care how much damage they did to the planet along the way. Wherever there was an ecological disaster, the Evilooters would never be far away. It was difficult to imagine what mischief they would get up to next. When Ling radioed the Beehive to tell them what they'd found, Ronan had something to tell them.

"Emile Dax is wanted by the police in six countries," he said. "He's a big game hunter and makes money by taking rich people on illegal hunting trips."

"So what's he doing in the Arctic?" asked Keira.

"The polar bears!" said Mo. "He's going to hunt polar bears."

"That's horrible," said Keira. "We have to stop him."

Then Ling spotted something.

"Look at this!" she said.

"Snowmobile tracks," said Keira.
"And look, there are patches of oil
here. One of the snowmobiles has a leak."

"Whoever was here must know about the missing bears," said Mo. "And I bet one of them was Emile Dax."

EVILOOTER CHARACTERS

PROFESSOR EMILE DAX

DECEPTION: 120

POLLUTING LEVEL: 62

CUNNING: 99

GREED: 108

ENVIRONMENTAL THREAT: 84

CHAPTER SEVEN
A STRANGE DISCOVERY

Following the snowmobile tracks
was easy, and it soon became easier
still. Up ahead, they saw a column

of smoke rising into the air. When they reached it, they found the smouldering remains of a snowmobile.

"This must be the one with a fuel leak," said Keira.

"It isn't Professor Dax's," said Mo. "It's much older than ours."

"Old vehicles like that cause lots of pollution," said Ling.

"Whoever was riding it can't be far away," said Mo. "We might still catch up with them."

"And look at this," said Keira, pointing at the front of the vehicle. "A logo of some kind."

"I'll send a picture to the Beehive," said Ling, taking out her camera. "Perhaps they can identify it."

★★★

Leaving the ruined snowmobile behind them, the friends carried on following the tracks. They appeared to be leading them towards a huge forest. Then Mo picked up another signal on the tracker.

"A red triangle," Mo said, excitedly. "And there's another one. That means people," said Keira.

"There's about a dozen of them," said Mo.

"That's strange," said Ling. "Karin said there were no other people for miles around."

"Here's something else that's strange," said Mo. "There's only two people now. The others just vanished." Up ahead, a narrow pathway lead into the forest. It was just wide enough for the snowmobiles.

"This way," said Ling, zooming off between the trees.

As Keira and Mo entered the forest they could see that Ling had come to a halt. When they reached her they could see why. A large area of the forest had been cleared of trees. And it looked as though it had only happened recently. The ground was covered with tree stumps and broken branches. A huge trailer stood to one side, piled high with freshly cut tree trunks.

"Chopping down trees also adds to greenhouse gases and causes global warming," said Ling. She explained that when plants grew, they

took in carbon dioxide. But when they were cut down, they released some of it back into the atmosphere.

"This doesn't look like the work of a big game hunter," said Keira. "Something much bigger is going on here."

Just then, Ling's radio crackled to life.

"I've managed to identify the logo on the snowmobile you found," said Ronan. "It belongs to the White Diamond Mining Company."

He told them the mine had been closed down years ago because of the damage that was being caused to the environment. Now, it was illegal to do any sort of mining in the area.

"We're going to find out what's going on," said Keira. "We've got our rucksacks so you should be able to keep track of us."

"I've got you on screen now," said Ronan. "You're not far from the old diamond mine, so be careful."

"And don't do anything silly," added Professor Darwin. "The police were interested to hear about Emile Dax. They're on their way as we speak."

Carefully avoiding the tree stumps, the team took their snowmobiles a bit further. It wasn't long before they discovered Ronan had been right about one thing. They were close to the diamond mine. But it didn't look old or abandoned at all.

Parking the snowmobiles behind a log pile, the three of them took off their helmets so they could take a better look. On one side was a row of log cabins with snowmobiles parked outside. Opposite them, stood a building with metal doors and barred windows.

"I wonder what they keep in there?" said Mo.

Further on they could see much larger buildings, and beyond them was the mine itself. From where they stood it just looked like an enormous hole in the ground.

"That's what I saw from the eco-booster," said Ling. "From above, it looked like some kind of giant wormhole."

"That explains the vanishing triangles on the tracker," said Mo. "The people must have gone down into the mine." Just then, a man stepped out of a cabin close by them. Luckily, he was heading the other way so hadn't spotted them.

From their hiding place, they watched the man make his way towards a cabin at the

glanced around then disappeared inside. Mo paused to look at one of the snowmobiles. "This is a new one like ours," he said. "Karin was right. Dax did take it."

When they reached the last cabin, they could hear the sound of voices coming from inside. Keira ducked beneath the window to listen.

"That looked like Emile Dax," said Mo. "Come on, let's see what he's up to." The three of them quickly made their way along the row of log cabins, their boots crunching in the snow.

CHAPTER EIGHT
UNCOVERING THE TRUTH

"It sounds like they're arguing," said Ling.

"I wish we could hear them properly," said Keira. She held her phone camera up to the window. "I can video-record them," she said. "We might be able to hear it better when we play it back."

While Keira was recording what was going on in the cabin, Ling noticed Mo looking at the tracking device with a frown. Then he started slowly walking towards the building with the big metal doors.

"Where are you going?" Ling whispered.

"There's something in there," Mo replied. "But the signal's very faint."

"Come back," begged Ling. But Mo wasn't listening. He was standing right in front of the metal doors, staring at the tracking device. There was definitely something inside. Two somethings by the look of it. But what were they?

Mo gave the door's handle a tug. With a deep groan it slid open slightly and Mo grinned – he'd expected it to be locked. Now he was about to find out what was inside.

"Mo!" came Ling's voice.

Looking around, Mo saw Ling and Keira frantically waving for him to come back. Then he saw why.

The door of the log cabin was open and Emile Dax was standing in the opening. If the man turned around he would see Mo instantly.

For a second, Mo stood frozen to the spot, wondering if he could make it back to his friends without being seen. But then his mind was made up for him.

Emile Dax had stepped outside and was just closing the cabin door behind him. Without another thought, Mo leapt through the doorway in front of him and dragged the door closed. The first thing he noticed, was how dark it was. The second thing was the smell. A rich, earthy smell. The sort he'd come across when visiting zoos or farms.

Mo glanced down at the tracker and saw two blue triangles. Then he heard a growl and the clank of metal on metal. Instinctively, he stepped back and felt his head bump against something on the wall. Lights flickered to life above his head and he realised it must have been a light switch.

The two polar bears were huddled together in a huge metal cage at the far end of the room.

Mo wanted to go over and set them free, but knew that wouldn't be a good idea. That was something that needed to be done very carefully.

With a loud groan, the metal door behind him suddenly opened wide. Ling and Keira stood there, smiling.

"You found them," said Ling. Keira was about to say something but the sound of her voice was drowned out by the noise of two police helicopters coming in to land.

Mo looked outside to see what was happening. As he did, he spotted Emile Dax and another man starting to race away on two snowmobiles.

"We've got to stop them," cried Mo. "They're going to get away."

"That's not why we're here," said Keira, putting a friendly hand on Mo's shoulder.

"Our mission was to find out what was happening to the polar bears," said Ling. "And that's what we've done."

"Yes, but ... " began Mo.

"Catching the criminals is for the professionals," said Keira.

★★★

Back at the Beehive, Mason Ash congratulated the Global Heroes on another successful mission.

"You'll be glad to hear that Emile Dax and some of the Evilooters were arrested by the police," he told them. "Unfortunately, their leader managed to get away."

"But what's the connection between Emile Dax, the polar bears and the diamond mine?" asked Mo.

Mason told them that opening up the old diamond mine was the biggest thing the Evilooters had attempted so far. "They thought no one would notice what they were up to in the Arctic," he said.

"Arvid and Karin told us there were no other people for miles around," said Ling. "The Evilooters must have thought they'd be left in peace to do what they wanted."

"That's right," said Mason Ash. "But they didn't count on hungry polar bears nosing around."

"Of course!" cried Mo. "Because the sea ice is forming later, the bears are wandering further inland. They're attracted to places where people live because they know there could be food there."

Mason explained that the Evilooters had recruited Dax to trap the bears and keep them away from the mine.

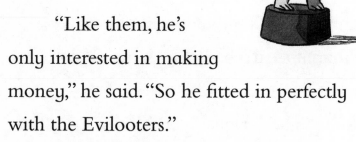

"Like them, he's only interested in making money," he said. "So he fitted in perfectly with the Evilooters."

Ronan explained that Dax found the bears with a tracker. He removed their ear tags so no one else could trace them. Then he planned to sell the bears as trophies to be hunted down by his rich friends.

"That's what Dax and the other Evilooters were arguing about in the cabin," said Ronan. "They thought Dax's little scheme could put the secrecy of the mine at risk."

"All the evidence is in the recording that Keira made," said Ronan. "That means we've successfully stopped another Evilooter plot."

"We've also managed to save two polar bears," said Mo.

"Make that three polar bears," added Professor Darwin. "Before releasing them, they discovered that the mother was pregnant. So that means you've helped increase the endangered population."

Mo smiled but still couldn't help feeling a little sad.

"We've found out it's not just global warming that's threatening polar bears in the wild," he said. "But it does seem that humans are at the bottom of everything."

"And it's not just polar bears that are being affected by global warming," said Ling. "It affects the whole world."

"Yes it does," said Mason Ash. "We're already received reports of rising water levels and widespread flooding in Madagascar."

"It sounds like our help will be needed," said Keira.

"You're right," said Mason Ash. "The Global Heroes need to be ready for the next adventure. The world clock is counting ... "

THE END

REGION PROFILE:

FAST FACTS:

* Most of the Arctic is ice (frozen ocean) rather than land

* The Arctic contains the North Pole which is the northernmost point on the planet

THE ARCTIC

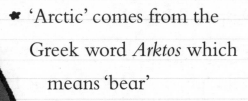

* 'Arctic' comes from the Greek word *Arktos* which means 'bear'

* The ice of the Arctic contains around ten per cent of the world's fresh water

* The Arctic covers an area of around 20 million km² (7.7 million square miles)

* The coldest recorded temperature in the Arctic is around −68 °C (−90 °F)

Despite the very cold climate, the Arctic is still home to lots of unique wildlife, including polar bears, Arctic foxes, Arctic hares and narwhals, as well as whales, seals and walruses.

POLAR BEAR FAST FACTS:

* The colour of a polar bear's fur is transparent – it looks white as it reflects light

* Polar bears have black skin underneath their fur to help absorb the Sun and keep warm

* They can swim very long distances

* They can smell their prey from far away, even underwater

* A group of polar bears is called a 'pack'

* They are the largest carnivores on land

* Polar bears give birth to their young in snow dens and stay there for 4-5 months

CLIMATE CHANGE:

The Earth is heating up due to climate change caused by activities such as burning fossil fuels.

CAUSE:

As the global temperatures rise, the polar ice is melting at an alarming rate. The Arctic ice cap is important for several reasons. The ice prevents the Arctic Ocean from losing heat. Snow-covered sea ice also reflects solar radiation back into the atmosphere.

EFFECT:

❧ Less ice means less absorption of the Sun's radiation

❧ Melting ice means the sea levels will rise and increase the risk of flooding

❧ Polar bears mostly hunt from the sea ice. With less sea ice, the polar bears may eventually run out of food which affects all of the food chain

But there is still time to help reduce the rate of ice caps melting.

FACT SHEET:

The world is getting warmer and weather more extreme because of human activity.

It's not too late to help look after the planet.

Little steps can make a big difference ...

Join the Global Heroes in their mission to protect Earth's future. Here are some ideas, but there is plenty more we can do!

CLIMATE ACTION

1) Reuse and recycle as much as you can to help reduce waste

2) Try making shorter journeys by foot, bike or scooter instead of by car

3) Keep electronic devices and lights turned off when not using them to reduce the energy you use

4) Join a tree-planting initiative in your local community

5) Use cold spin cycles or eco settings on washing machines

6) Join a conservation team or sponsor an endangered animal

QUIZ

1) What is the name of the suits the team wear in the cold?

2) Where do Mo and Ling travel to?

3) What caused a chunk of ice to fall off the glacier?

4) What are 'bergy bits'?

5) What does Mo lose in the ice?

6) What do the team discover in a clearing?

7) What does Mo discover inside the mine?

GLOSSARY

CARBON EMISSIONS – harmful waste gases from planes, cars, factories, etc

CARNIVORE – meat eater

CURRENT – the movement of sea water

ECOLOGY – relationship between living things and their environments

FUEL – substance burned to create heat or energy (fossil fuels are coal, oil or gas)

GAME HUNTER – person who hunts wild animals

GROWLER – a small iceberg

GREENHOUSE EFFECT – the warming up of the Earth

HABITAT – the place that an animal lives in

ICEBERG – large section of ice floating in the ocean

MICROPHONE – device that transports and amplifies sound

POISON – dangerous substance which causes harm

PROFIT – to make money from selling something for more than it cost

REFUELLING – to add more fuel to something so it can move again

SIGNAL – a motion, action, movement or sound to communicate something

SNOWMOBILE – motorised vehicle that travels on snow or ice

WASTE – things that are thrown away

GLOBAL HEROES

JOIN THE GLOBAL HEROES TEAM IN THESE FANTASTIC ADVENTURES:

9781445180953

9781445182988

9781445182964

9781445182971